I0842993

ZACH'S HEART

EVERYONE DESERVES LOVE

Debra Bauguess

Zach's Heart

Copyright © 2024 by Debra Bauguess

ISBN: 978-1962497985(hc)
ISBN: 978-1962497978(sc)
ISBN: 978-1962497992(e)

All rights reserved. No part of this publication may be reproduced, distributed, or transmitted in any form or by any means, including photocopying, recording, or other electronic or mechanical methods, without the prior written permission of the publisher and/or the author, except in the case of brief quotations embodied in critical reviews and other noncommercial uses permitted by copyright law.

The views expressed in this book are solely those of the author and do not necessarily reflect the views of the publisher, and the publisher hereby disclaims any responsibility for them.

The Reading Glass Books
(888) 420-3050
www.readingglassbooks.com
fulfillment@readingglassbooks.com

RN

Once there was a young man named Zach. His whole name was Zachary, but his beloved Grandpa Luke called him Zach, so he liked that best. Zach's parents were hardworking, honest, loving people. His mom was an RN in an ICU and his dad worked for the forest service. All who met them loved their gentle caring ways. They'd always had pets and Zach grew up loving nature and helping people and animals. He loved that his dad helped protect the forest and its amazing variety of animals. He loved that his mom hugged everyone she met, and she cared deeply about each and every one of them. He grew to love the beautiful giant majestic trees of the deep woods, the tiny chipmunks that frittered to and fro, and the gurgling creeks constantly splashing over boulders on their way to the lakes. He loved the overwhelming beauty of the snowcapped peak of the nearby mountain. They had deep faith in the Creator that made this beautiful planet and its animals. They were a part of a loving, thriving church and they prayed each night, together before bed.

They were happy as a family and were an integral part of the mountain community they lived in. Zach's parents each worked full time, so he spent much of his spare time and summers helping his Grandfather around his farm. Grandpa Luke had several acres with a large barn, garden area and 8 bedroom rambling farmhouse. The house had a walk around porch, large kitchen, old rock fireplace and a large family area. Grandpa Luke, as did Zach's parents, believed deeply in God and had great faith. They'd all raised Zach to understand that every life, human or animal is precious in the creator's eyes. They all had purpose. Zach loved caring for the farm animals, helping with preparing the earth for planting, harvesting the produce, and doing the odd construction or "fix-it" job on the farm. His grandpa was a "Jack of all trades" as was his father and grandfather before him. Grandpa Luke even taught Zach to cook. His folks were actually amazed by how much Zach was learning about so many different things.

Grandpa Luke believed in giving back what you are blessed by God with, so he frequently gave away extra vegetables to less fortunate neighbors. He and Zach would help others whenever a field needed tilling or a house needed repair. Luke's large barn became a haven and healing ground for Grandpa Luke and Zach to care for injured, hurting neighborhood pets, forest animals and strays. Grandpa Luke laid hands on and prayed over everything he touched, believing God's healing power flowed into all he prayed for.

Zach became Grandpa Luke's second hand man and grew strong, full of great empathy, caring and honesty - a wonderful blend of his parents and his Grandfather. Zach worked hard on the farm and also took on many paid jobs around town, building and fixing old stores and homes. He started to notice different people around town that needed help. He would lend a hand, food or money every time he could.

One day, Zach, now 20 years old, noticed his Grandpa looking tired. By the time Zach was 22; his Grandpa Luke had passed away peacefully in his sleep - leaving his entire farm and house to Zach. Zach and his parents missed Grandpa Luke deeply, but also knew he was with the Lord, in Heaven waiting for them. Zach felt a great responsibility to Grandpa Luke to follow his Grandfather's teachings. He believed everyone had worth and all animals and humans were useful, important and loved by God. Zach's parents were thrilled their loving son would now have his own home and life's work to look forward to.

Zach got busy and cleaned and repaired and painted the house from top to bottom. He made each room a place of unique sanctuary and peace. There were about 7 bedrooms, not including his master suite, which had huge windows overlooking the nearby forest. You could even hear the song of the nearby creek at night, with windows open. The barn got scrubbed and repainted with many new stalls and enclosures, made for all sizes of animals.

VIETNAM
VET
HOLY
BIBLE

Grandpa Luke had left a large amount of savings for Zach for upkeep, and for helping "those less fortunate". He believed in "giving back" to those who could not help themselves. Zach, now, surveyed his property and felt peace, but felt a little lonely. It felt empty. He went to the pound, the next day and picked out a pup, a golden retriever he named Brandy and an orange striped kitten he named Scooters. He was happy, but felt a "tug" from God to "reach out" and "bring in those that are hurting". He prayed hard about exactly what this meant and started to see new ideas in his mind.

The next day, he walked downtown and "saw" a homeless man on the corner. He was a Vet and had fought in Vietnam. He'd been injured in a bombing and had lost one leg below the knee. He looked sad, tired and like he'd given up on the compassion of strangers. His sign said, he'd do any job for food. Zach asked his name, it was Ken. He said, "I have a room you can stay in, if you help me with chores and cooking; if you like, please come". Ken wearily stood, using his prosthetic leg, straightened himself and said, "Is this for real, son?" Zach said, "Yes, sir, as long as you rest, heal, eat all you want and help me around the farm". Ken suddenly developed a sparkle in his eyes as a tear seeped out. He held out his hand and shook Zach's hand. That night, in a soft, warm bed, after a hot shower and bowl of stew, Ken drifted off into a trouble free sleep in his very own room facing the mountain. The sunset glowed on the snow cap, turning it pink and orange. Ken's dreams were peaceful and untroubled for the first time in many years.

A few days later, Zach passed by a dirty, lanky teenager pushing a shopping cart full of belongings. A gray striped 3 legged cat sat on top. The young man looked hungry. Zach stopped in front of him and said, "Young man, do you have a family or home?" The teen, Peter, said, "No sir, I was just released from the orphanage since I'm 18 now, and am on my own, no family or home." Zach said, "You have a family now, if you choose. I have a room for you in a farm house, but you need to keep up your room and help out with my Grandfather's farm." Peter said, "I can't believe this, I will work hard for you to have food and shelter and a place to call home. I love animals and used to help a veterinarian, do you need help with caring for any of your animals?" Zach said, "Absolutely, we have pets, farm animals and sometimes a stray, injured forest critter". Peter straightened up and smiled from ear to ear and said, "I'm ready, let's go, can I bring my cat, MacGyver?" Zach said, "Sure, let's go". Peter fell into a deep peaceful sleep that night in his own warm bed. He was clean, with a full tummy and felt needed- for the first time in his life.

Zach, Peter and Ken fell into a comfortable routine and became great friends. Peter spent much of his time in the barn, caring for his animal friends, while he voraciously read books on animal care, hoping to become a vet someday. Ken read cook books and decided he loved cooking. He tried many new recipes on his new friends, all of which were delicious. He really had a gift for different flavors and fresh taste.

Zach read about a woman in her 30's, with Down's syndrome that had lived with her folks, but her folks had suddenly died. This woman now had no family to live with. He went to the new conservator of the young woman and asked to meet her. Kendra was lovely and sweet and very responsible. She told Zach she loved all growing things and had cared for her parent's yard and large garden, producing many vegetables. The sale of her parents' house had left her well off, but she needed to live with someone who could look out for her. Zach asked her and the conservator if he could be responsible for her and have her live at his home. She would be able to grow flowers and vegetables in his large garden. She jumped up and down and said, "Oh please, Oh please, may I?" The conservator filed the proper paper work and thanked Zach. She fell asleep that night in a cheerful room facing the very large garden, watching the birds flit from flower to flower. She had the biggest smile on her face and felt happy. The house soon had vases of bright flowers and Ken had all the fresh vegetables he could even dream of cooking with. Ken even cooked up special animal worthy, healing foods that Peter's barnyard animals thrived on.

Zach then met a young woman Cheri that was going to lose her apartment. She'd had an extended illness and had lost her job. He told Cheri, "I have an open room in a large house, for you to live in, as long as you help out with chores around the house". Her eyes let up, filled with hope. She felt something open and honest in Zach. She said, "Is there a catch to this?" Zach said, "My Grandfather taught me to help those that need it and that God would point them out to me". "I feel that you need a break in life". Cheri said, "Thank you, from the bottom of my heart, but I do have a daughter, she's 7; is she welcome?" Zach said, "Of course, I have the perfect room for you two".

Cheri and her daughter, Patty, walked into a large, bright double sized room with windows facing gardens on one side and a mountain on the other. One large bed with a beautiful mirrored vanity and sitting area by the mountain was hers, while Patty had a bed facing the beautiful gardens, with a play area and large bookshelf, full of books. She even had a window ledge with stuffed animals all in a row, in the sunshine. Cheri noticed a piano in the main family room and asked Zach's permission to play it. She had studied for many years. He said he'd be delighted. She sat down and played and all nearby came to stand and listen. It was joy filled. She knew all the hymns and worship songs and many silly, happy songs as well.

Cheri became a great help to Ken in his cooking and she also delighted in keeping the house clean and beautiful. Little Patty became the avid helper of Peter in his work helping the animals. She named them all, whether alive or stuffed. There was Zorro, Angel, Dandelion, Mr. Blue, Fooey, Lily, Whiskers, Muffin, Mikey, etc. Each one fit his/her name and was special to Peter and Patty. Mr. Blue, a part Siamese kitty, had such beautiful blue eyes and followed her everywhere, like a puppy. MacGyver was her favorite; he'd lost a leg in an accident and had no problem hopping all around the barn and yard chasing butterflies on 3 legs. Angel would meow and "talk" all the time and always hid behind things with her little glowing green eyes and all black soft coat. Angel slept on a pillow, covered by a soft blanket with her in bed at night and meowed back to her every time Patty would lift the blanket and say "I love you".

One day, a man knocked on the door and asked if they needed any work done or had any odd projects he could get paid for as he was down on his luck. Zach had him come in for a hearty lunch and found out that Alex had learned carpentry skills from his dad and had an artistic streak from his mom. He loved to create gadgets, and fix things. He was in between low paying jobs. Zach said, "I'll give you a choice, stay here, help us in the up keep of barn and house, and I'll feed you and shelter you. " Alex's eyes opened wide and he said, "Why would you do this for a stranger?" Zach said, "I'm a good judge of people's hearts and I feel you have a good one. You are welcome to join our family. " Alex fell asleep that night listening to the wind in the fir and pine trees, after finding great company in the farm house group and great comfort from the fresh garden food. Little Patty kept telling Alex the names of all her "pets" in the barn, and asked if he'd read her a good night story. Alex felt unconditional love for the first time in a very long time. Alex also discovered a part of the barn that was full of Grandpa Luke's old junk and broken farm equipment pieces. He soon started creating unique sculptures that danced in the breeze around the farm. He enjoyed fixing broken things and giving them new life. He kept the house and barn painted and in good repair.

MILK
FLOUR
SUGAR

One day, at lunch in a downtown Bakery, Zach noticed a waitress, Becky, who looked distressed. He asked if she was ok and she said she had her hours cut and couldn't afford her rent anymore. Zach looked thoughtful and then asked if she'd like to start afresh in a houseful of like people, where love ruled. He told her she'd have a cozy room, food and a new caring family if she helped around the house. She looked astonished and said, "How can this be?" Zach said, "Come with me and I'll show you ". Becky's room was right above the large farm house kitchen, facing each morning's sunrise. The smell of flowers and fresh made bread wafted up to her each morning. She'd never felt so at peace. She started baking pastries with Ken each AM and then found she liked to paint. She'd always loved it, but had little opportunity to dabble in it. Soon the side of the barn and walls in the house in each room had soft, surreal landscapes in peaceful shades that reflected each person's likes and loves in nature. Little Patty's wall had flowers and little animals hiding and playing in glorious color.

After a time, Ken was teaching neighborhood children to cook and giving all extra food and meals to food banks and the homeless. He had lost his haggard look and skinniness. He looked healthy and smiled all the time. A couple of abandoned labs, one a yellow one he named Honey, and one a black one he named Shasta, became his special pets. They fetched sticks and balls and swam in the creek and made him laugh. Brandy, the retriever, used to try and stuff 2-3 tennis balls in her mouth and loved leaping in the creek with Honey and Shasta. They loved his homemade dog biscuits.

Peter lavished love, with Patty's help on each animal and was finishing his studies to be a vet. The barn was at times, overflowing with healing, happy creatures, that knew someone loved and cared for them. Even people from town asked advice and brought their sick animals to be healed. Peter and Patty became like brother and sister. All who walked into that barn felt unconditional love and had any number of animals call out to them to be given attention and petted. Peter loved all the animals, but Whiskers and Scooters were always by his side, either in his lap when he rested or following him anywhere he went. 5 other little dogs, Muffin, Kukla, Poco, Happy and Daisy ran up to each child that ever visited and jumped all over them, the children dissolving in giggles. They all eventually got adopted and had forever homes in town. Peter didn't believe in the dogs staying in the local animal shelter, so he took them to his barn, and lavished love on them and fed them nutritious food until they each found homes.

Kendra never felt "different" again and grew flowers and veggies and fruit many had never seen or tasted before. The garden was glorious and people from town came to wander through it to find peace. The local Nursery would save special seeds from exotic, faraway plants to give her. She loved the barn, too. There so many furry critters to hug and spend time with. Kendra especially loved the little black and white kitty, Lily. She had a white stripe down the front of her head and face and 4 white paws. She had showed up one day with a badly hurt paw, got tended to and now sat on Kendra's chest, up by her neck, because she wanted to feel Kendra's heartbeat. Kendra felt the purring of Lily in her ear and it soothed her like nothing else could. Cheri loved Kendra like her own sister and they became very close. When Cheri played worship music, Kendra would sit and soak up the soothing love pouring out from her Father above. Kendra bloomed internally and was always smiling. Her glorious colorful garden reflected the love she felt. Alex had several whimsical metal chairs to sit in, among the flowers, to soak up the beauty and feel peace.

Cheri taught piano lessons to town folk and played worship songs on Sundays and Carols at Christmas. The house was full of joy and sweet music day and night. Even the animals liked the music. Cheri would have a "house cleaning day" once a week and everyone helped. They all did their own rooms and each took one other part of the house. It would only take them part of a day to make it smell fresh and shine with love. They would then have a picnic outside somewhere beautiful; on the porch or in the barn, if it rained. Zorro, the gray striped kitty chose her and slept stretched out beside her at night.

Alex kept everything in tip top shape and soon sold his creations all over town. He showed anyone that wanted to learn how to make their own special artistic creations. He fell in love with a Golden retriever that was a stray and named her Melina. He then took in a part retriever part bulldog, he named Onyx. They were hilarious together, tugging on the same chew toy and mock fighting for hours. They also swam in any creek swimming hole they found, until they were exhausted. Alex's love for Jesus shone out of him, in his manner and all he touched.

Becky went from making flaky, buttery pastry dough in the AM to landscape painting on town buildings and on walls in town homes. Her gentle use of nature and color in her murals brought peace and beauty to all who saw it. It was like nature was flowing into people's homes through her art and vision. She had a class once a week to teach any who wanted to dabble, draw, paint or create. The local hardware store opened a section of artwork made by local children and visitors came from far and wide to buy it. The big orange tabby, Dandelion, and black cat named Fooey, chose Becky to follow around. They loved the garden and loved to help her paint, often ending up with paws of various colors for a time.

The animals all thrived on the good food, care and love they received from so many. They seemed to sense that this was a safe place and they would not get hurt or be hungry. Each animal seemed to "pick" a different person in the house or another animal to lavish love on. It didn't even matter if they were the same species. An older momma dog took care of any orphaned baby critter that found its way to them. A donkey, a lamb and a calf became a trio that gambled around spreading trouble and cheer. Squirrels, skunks and possums hung out with the barn animals. There were always silly, crazy antics going on around the barn. Peter and Patty had their hands full, but loved it.

Zach's parents were so proud. Grandpa Luke's legacy had birthed a thriving, loving community where all who gave, were given back the healing power of love, family and a feeling of purpose. They each felt "needed" and a part of something bigger than themselves. The power of love from a God who wishes for a relationship with us and loves us with a mighty everlasting love – overcame any hardship they went through. They prayed with and for each other, they became "family" and they were all happy, fulfilled and eager to share that love with others. The eighth empty room was there for the next person down on their luck that needed a home, food, love and a place to feel needed. Many town folk would come to the house just to sit in the garden or play with the dogs and other animals. Once a month they would all gather for a bonfire and worship out between the garden and the barn. Their praises would rise up the Heavens and the Angels would join in. The animals in the barn would drift off to sleep lulled by many voices thanking a very Real God for His love, hope and promise.

As they sat around the large dining table and gave thanks to God each night, they felt peace and joy. Each one of them, including Zach, felt contentment and like life had given them a fresh start. Accidents and troubles still happened but the prayer and faith in a caring God made everything hard, bearable. They had each other, all ages, with different strengths and weaknesses under one roof to turn to when a hug or shoulder to cry on was needed. It started with God and grew to a Grandfather, his grandson, and now a home and entire town – changed by the power of unconditional love. Zach's Grandpa looked down on him from Heaven, so very proud of his grandson.

www.ingramcontent.com/pod-product-compliance
Lightning Source LLC
Chambersburg PA
CBHW041415300726

48978CB00002B/102